# CHRISTMAS CATS

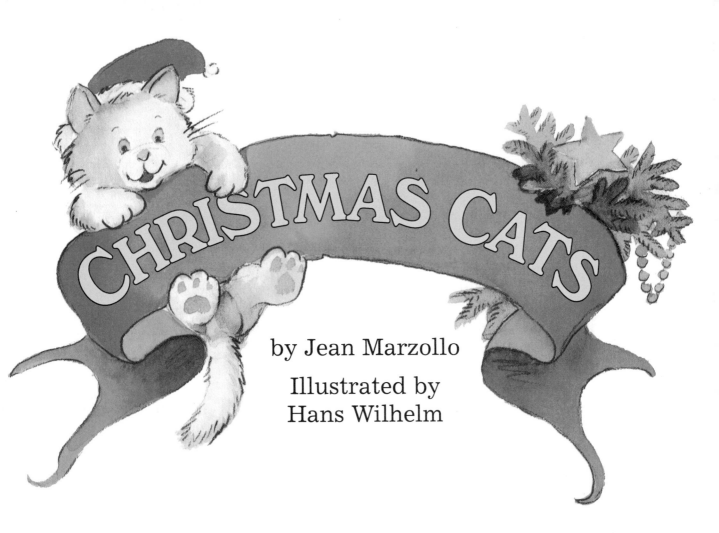

# CHRISTMAS CATS

by Jean Marzollo

Illustrated by
Hans Wilhelm

Cartwheel
·B·O·O·K·S·®

SCHOLASTIC INC.
New York   Toronto   London   Auckland   Sydney

Library of Congress Cataloging-in-Publication Data

Marzollo, Jean.
    Christmas cats / by Jean Marzollo; illustrated by Hans Wilhelm.
      p.  cm.
    "Cartwheel books."
    Summary: Creative cats prepare for Christmas by making chains, hanging mistletoe, and singing carols.
    ISBN 0-590-37212-2  (alk. paper)
    [1.  Cats —Fiction.  2.  Christmas —Fiction.  3.  Stories in rhyme.]
I.  Wilhelm, Hans, ill.    II.  Title.
PZ8.3.M4194Ch   1997
[E]—dc21
                                                                              97-7213
                                                                                   CIP
                                                                                    AC

10  9  8  7  6  5  4  3  2  1

Printed in the U.S.A.                        24
First printing, November 1997

*For the Fausts: five cool Christmas cats*

— J.M.

Christmas cats make lists.

Christmas cats plan, too.

Christmas cats hunt around

for paper, clay, and glue.

Christmas cats make presents:

a mat, a bowl, a drum.

*Little kittens asking,*
  *"When will Santa Cat come?"*

Christmas cats make chains.

They hang the mistletoe.

Christmas cats light windows.

Christmas cats roll dough.

Christmas cats clean up

every little drop and crumb.

*Little kittens asking,*
*"When will Santa Cat come?"*

Christmas cats wrap presents.

Christmas cats tie bows.

Christmas cats sing

as the snowy wind blows.

Christmas cats dream

while they sleep. "Yum, Yum!"

Little kittens shouting,
"Look! Santa Cat has come!"

# Merry Christmas!